AF261543

LINGHEART
PUBLISHING

LONGING

LINGHEART PUBLISHING

Lingheart Publishing preserves and experiments with different forms and perspectives in English language and literature. It furthers this objective to enlighten readers by exploring subjects that are a crucial part of the millennium age.

Published in the United Kingdom by Lingheart Publishing, Portsmouth.

Lingheart speciesism edition published in September 2019 (Lingheart Publishing).

This edition of the text was edited and proofread for the speciesism collection. The content within this book is the sole property of Lingheart Publishing and are for personal or academic use only. Copyright 2019, Lingheart Publishing.

My future love. I found this journal
and I know it is going to be a special
part of my life until you arrive.
This is my honesty in my highest
and lowest moments. I come to you
with the highest light in my heart.
My heart is part of you and will be
forever. You mean more to me
than you could ever imagine. I long
for you with all of my heart. I suffer
and suffer and suffer and suffer.
I suffer with all of me until we are
one again. I love you. I love you
so much. I am saving myself for you.
So lonely as I feel your human absence
but feel your energy reaching out to me
somewhere in the future. I must be
patient. I long for you and it makes me
weep. I know that my heart beams
and through that beam I can receive
some of your everlasting essence.
My invisible heart. Always and forever.
I only know that you exist out there

24 somewhere. No more. No less. Endless.

25 I care about you in a way that worries

26 me. I care about you more than

27 anything on this planet. It makes me

28 feel terribly guilty. But you. You are

29 hypnotic and once I have a sense

30 of your energy I am lost in a trance.

31 The essence of you alone

32 could save me a thousand times over.

33 These moments of words

34 bring my mind into peace. I miss you.

35 I long for you. I cannot help but repeat

36 the sirens in my mind. I need you

37 so much and you are not here. I cannot

38 bear it. I believe that everything happens

39 in divine timing. I know there is purpose

40 to this and I will allow myself to feel

41 and flow through your painful absence.

42 I wish you were holding me so tightly

43 with every fibre of your being. Your

44 embrace could cure every pain

45 in the universe and your words

46 could soothe a thousand nights of pain

and death. I could live forever

with just the touch of your hand

over my skin or between the crevices

of my hand that is only part of you.

I am you and you are me. You are me.

Every part of me. I am you. I am you

with all of everything. I cannot bear

this missing part of me. I cannot reach

you in physical form. I could be dead.

The only beat I should know is yours

and I do not know it at all. I feel

incompetent. I feel worthless.

I miss you. I feel wrong. I feel

so wrong. This must be right. Being

without you right now must be right.

Meaning. But this hurts tremendously.

My heart weeps for you. I am not

thinking clearly. Everything feels absent

and numb of thought. I have to confess

that it is unbearable. I do not know how

I am surviving. I am barely alive.

My brain feels dead.

I want to scream your name and find you

70 with my expression of pain. But I cannot

71 scream and I do not know your name.

72 I need you now. I cannot do this. I cannot

73 do this. I cannot do this. Why

74 does the universe do this to me? Why

75 does the universe keep me away

76 from you? The pain of losing you

77 every single moment that I live

78 is truly unbearable. You never leave

79 my mind. But even for a moment I will

80 never forget you even though I cannot

81 remember you. Why did you leave me

82 here alone in this existence

83 where I crave you so much to the point

84 of the edge. You left me here on this

85 endless edge. What made you think

86 I was strong enough? Some days

87 I wonder how my body can still function

88 when half of it is lost somewhere in time.

89 We are both essentially one person

90 and we somehow manage to function

91 apart from one another. This detachment

92 is powerful and relentless but despite

93 the deep murdering magnetism

94 we can make a life for ourselves in this

95 world with half a heartbeat. This heartbeat

96 feels abstract and not part of reality

97 as my reality is knowing that my heart

98 is severed in two. If anything I can feel

99 the blood and hear the blood as it bleeds

100 out of an empty energy and flows

101 toward the other side of itself

102 in a torturous loop of forever seeking.

103 The days are feeling calm and I think

104 of you now as a neverending part

105 of my life that coexists next to me

106 at all times and stages of mental clarity

107 and fear. The love in my heart feels

108 warm and justified. Your essence feels

109 pure and open to receiving and giving

110 me signals that can expand far greater

111 than just the two of us. We are part

112 of this great existence and we contribute

113 by living a life that moves

114 with purposeful seeking and expansion

115 of the mind, body, and heart. One

116   of the same. All of the same. I feel

117   a twinkling in my heart that evaporates

118   up and outward into the universe.

119   Perhaps this twinkling longs to be heard

120   through every sense of life and matter.

121   Perhaps your heart is twinkling

122   as I weep as it is getting rather past

123   the will of time. I am your future

124   looking back into the past as we both

125   wait for this divine union to be as it is

126   meant to be. I think about you now

127   as I reach a time in my life

128   where I observe creation in awe

129   and wonder and fantasise

130   about what all are going to create

131   in this world. Their individual beauty

132   and curious nature only inspires

133   me more as I look into our future.

134   They are a glimpse of an evolutionary

135   story, and a never-ending one at that.

136   I do believe and pray that one day I will

137   be capable of being a maternal energy

138   to those growing beings that stumble

139 upon this world and learn to walk

140 in more ways than one. You also

141 teach others how to walk as you

142 take in information and make it new

143 through your perception. I wonder

144 what you will create next. I wonder

145 what we will create next. I wonder

146 how I am wondering and believing

147 in our future at all when my mind feels

148 so torn and lost in an abyss

149 that seems as neverending

150 as the beauty of nature and future

151 expansion. The reason I long for you

152 is because as time passes by the world

153 becomes more loving and understanding

154 coming to an equilibrium. I do

155 not want to witness this without you

156 and sometimes I wonder

157 if the world will change at all without you.

158 I believe that every single person here

159 can make an impact. You and I

160 are capable of spreading love to the ends

161 of the earth until it bursts out

162   into the universe. I believe and I know

163   in my heart that it will happen. It hurts

164   to deprive the world of love. Every speckle

165   of love is extremely important, if

166   not essential. You are essential. I cannot

167   do this without you. It is too much

168   to bear with my hands alone. The world

169   is an overwhelming place with many

170   injustices that crucify my ethics and morals.

171   I am but a dead being that has died over

172   and over again in that dreary and torturous

173   gas chamber or cold floor that I was

174   either left to die on or faced as I dangled

175   upside down. I bled out again and again

176   as just the number behind the name

177   that may have not existed in the first place

178   because my sensibilities dismissed

179   that I was anything more than what

180   they defined me to be. I was not even

181   a number, as much as I was

182   an encompassment of every other

183   single being like me. The most

184   terrifying connotation behind the word

185 product is that it can be applied
186 to anything and suddenly take
187 away everything at the same time.
188 I long for you. I do so much to the ends
189 of all of this madness and back. I cannot
190 bear to even do this without you.
191 I feel like I am experiencing all
192 the deaths of the world at once
193 on a neverending loop of pain
194 and suffering. Pain and suffering.
195 These two words are the only words
196 that can even survive or exist during this
197 time. How can we even say any more
198 words to one another when we bear
199 witness to such pain and suffering
200 without it coming to an end in the here
201 and now. In that very moment, in the here
202 and now, always and forever it still exists
203 in this incomprehensible conditioned
204 nightmare. I wonder how I will be able
205 to dig into your mind and comprehend
206 you as a being. I know that there is
207 a deeper connection to the universe

208   that can define us all almost

209   to the point where we know

210   someone without knowing them at all.

211   Our life is seemingly written

212   and therefore I will always meet you

213   whenever I am granted the pleasure

214   of finally meeting you as the

215   beautiful energy you are and did

216   bring to this planet. It is like I have

217   discovered your existence now even if

218   my perspective of you is in the future.

219   Time is fluid. My soul feels the future

220   as though I have already lived through it

221   and depending on the meaning

222   of the world, it could be said

223   that everything exists in this one moment.

224   Time goes by and I feel you more

225   and more. Your energy is so profound

226   that it keeps me alive. My heart means

227   more than I could ever know when

228   it is surrounded your everlasting unifying

229   boundless essence. Your soul is my soul.

230   We are a neverending soul. The bounds

231   that we place on our love are only

232   bound to human existence in this level

233   of consciousness. We can transcend

234   that together with our beautiful love

235   as it moves past and analyses and transcends

236   any obstacle that comes before us. We will

237   change existence into a whole being

238   that is only ever one and only ever

239   whole. This will be to such existence

240   of tyranny or deception of the masses

241   as we see through and penetrate

242   the energy with our eternal love that will

243   spread and manifest itself in the vision

244   of those yet to evolve to their highest

245   form of awareness that will only grow

246   and exceed all levels of consciousness.

247   We are all one. We are the microcosm

248   of the world. We are here to give

249   to the world and receive the world. I love

250   you endlessly. I feel sometimes

251   that I die over and over again just to become

252   closer to you because every time

253   I die I get to experience what it is

254   to truly need you. Each time my life shatters

255   I scream for you to pick up the pieces.

256   I scream for you to soothe the pain

257   and it brings me closer to you. I hurt

258   because you are not here and it is

259   that hurt that tells me how much I need you

260   to come back to me from the higher

261   source in this lifetime. I am truly

262   exhausted. I long for you over and over

263   again. I want to write those words

264   over and over again. I long for you.

265   I long for you. I long for you. I long

266   for you. I long for you. I long for you.

267   I long for you. I feel worthless. I feel

268   pathetic. I feel as though I am

269   collapsing into myself and smashing

270   into billions of pieces and then trying

271   to put myself back together again.

272   The pieces are all muddled

273   and they somehow fit together

274   to form a figure of what should exist.

275   If only you existed in my reality.

276   This love hurts because it is

277 too much to bear for one person.

278 The feeling is so immense that I want

279 to not exist and let it exist in itself.

280 But no matter how I exist on this

281 world, I know I want to exist with you.

282 I am you. I will focus on writing

283 tomorrow and the day after and the day

284 after and the day after. The writing

285 will be about expressing my love to you

286 and when I look into your soul

287 through your eyes, I will express

288 this love. This all-consuming love

289 that could destroy us both and transcend

290 us at the same time. I will always

291 look up to you and dream of you

292 in every moment. I think of you always

293 and I cannot stop this hypnotism.

294 Love is the reason I am alive. You

295 existing is enough for me to want to stay

296 here and be with you in this world. This

297 world needs love. Everyone needs love.

298 You are love. I feel I should come

299 to you with all of me and at all times

300 when I feel an urge to express love.

301 I want to translate the feeling

302 of your touch into words that are

303 more permanent than human form.

304 However, I do wonder how it feels

305 to fall into wonder within your being

306 and feel safe in that moment as I transcend

307 my consciousness into the mystery.

308 The dreams my being creates without

309 my surface. I feel once these words

310 pass I should not read them.

311 I should only create more.

312 I would be neglecting you if I chose

313 to pause for a moment and disconnect

314 from you. I want to feel all of you

315 as one with me. I want you to merge

316 with me. I want to be you. I want you

317 to be me. Maybe we should forget

318 the word want and instead say need

319 because love is too intentional

320 to mention the word want. I need you.

321 I have to open this book even when I close it

322 because I want you here so much

323 in this tiny moment of existence. You are

324 here but where you are is somewhere.

325 If I open these pages, I am bursting

326 with the essence of your love and then I

327 close it only to feel that irresistible temptation

328 again to open up the overflowing love

329 that pours through us both and manifests

330 within the white, blank space that is now

331 full but still filling. I may feel deeply

332 alone but home is right here in these pages.

333 Your energy is pulling me inside these

334 pages and I feel every time I give in

335 I disappear in an abstract bliss of all that is

336 to be created in the movements forward

337 and the thoughts that flow through me

338 when I fantasise about your energy.

339 Maybe if I stare at you long enough,

340 you will manifest yourself energetically

341 right in front of me like sparkles

342 of existence not yet formed in this

343 time-space. I wonder if your heart would

344 drop like mine in this moment. I wonder

345 if I should try to create what is

the most freeing aspect of life. Creating
of creating. If I can write properly,
creating your existence could make this
experience less unconditional.
The unconditional aspects could make
me wait an entire lifetime to discover
you. And I could not discover you at all
and die alone in this world without you.
It would be worth it to know I remained
faithful to you in our soul marriage
outside of this world. I am reaching
out to you with both hands and I
cannot feel you other than the soft
calling of love in the future. I know
that this book is nothing compared
to you and I wonder if
my pathetic attempts as perhaps this
seems it would be perceived
would meet anything outside myself.
I think this is beautiful but in my thoughts
there lingers things of ongoing criticism
that tell me I cannot express myself
in a raw and vulnerable way without

369 being subject to falling hard

370 in the opposite direction of falling

371 for you. I feel weak. I feel exhausted.

372 I feel unable to function

373 because of your love. It wounds me

374 to the point where I cannot open

375 my eyes. They feel heavy and deep.

376 That deepness becomes part of

377 the heavy. Almost as if my eyes are

378 carrying an overbearing and absent

379 amount of water that is too vast

380 to comprehend. I could fall.

381 My body is trying to tell me to fall

382 as my eyes find this too much to bear.

383 They cannot hold the weight of this water

384 and it does not move but inadvertently

385 thrashes like all consuming waves

386 to find itself within my mind. I am

387 exhausted. I cannot move much

388 and my brain is not moving either.

389 To write at more length would be

390 the overrule conceptual meaning

391 behind taking a heavy breath. I cannot

392 move my hand. I cannot think.

393 I am shutting down for love. I know

394 I should keep writing but it becomes

395 unbearable right now. I give to you

396 by giving in to my vulnerable body

397 and falling. I cannot give to you

398 by writing. The exhaustion itself

399 must show you how much I need you.

400 You are my paralysis. Your absence

401 conveys the absence of all love.

402 The world could be an empty

403 space that bears no purpose.

404 The idea of that is terrifying

405 as I believe everything has a hidden

406 meaning. Everything that can exist

407 in one sense or another comes

408 to being for a reason. I came here

409 meaning to be with you. I came here

410 knowing that my true meaning was

411 entangled with the world. I am not

412 sure I can function without you

413 and if I cannot function then how

414 can the world I perceive function

415   without each perception of it evolving

416   and growing. I am not therefore part

417   of the world as it continuously spins

418   without you. I am desolate. I am

419   an observer of what is rather than

420   what I so desperately want it to become.

421   I am violated from all that makes love

422   boundless in this unintentional stagnation.

423   The path I bear in front of me cannot be

424   journeyed without faith. Faith surrounds

425   all that I must convey. My heart does

426   not die and this faith cannot subside.

427   I need patience but how can patience

428   have a place in a world where there is

429   continuous suffering and death.

430   You must know the importance of love

431   in this terrifying place we all call home.

432   I found enlightenment

433   and I had to feel you close. I feel

434   like you left me without saying goodbye.

435   I could have had you for a moment

436   that felt like my entire life

437   only to lose you when I opened

438   my eyes. I should not have left you.

439   I should have kept calling out

440   for you until you manifested in

441   a way that was forever. The silence

442   tells my heart that this reality is without

443   you. My heart refuses to bear that truth

444   without your soul comforting the lies

445   that surround it. There is only you.

446   The refusal of a life with you would be

447   the refusal that life exists. Life is not

448   a lie. I wonder what we would do

449   together if we were one. I wonder

450   how the impossible would feel. I am

451   faithful to longing. I am faithful

452   to the pain. I am faithful to the hope.

453   My heartbeat feels you, but it is

454   hiding underneath a body that does not.

455   I could listen for the beats or place my

456   hand on my chest and feel nothing.

457   I am denying myself of a heart.

458   I am holding It back because it is

459   too fragile to live. I must live.

460   I have to live. I understand the immense

461 feeling and what that feeling can

462 create. Every being shares a purpose

463 here. I need you. Your body binds

464 with mine and I cannot live

465 as this wound keeps bleeding. I wonder

466 how I am not dead. I wonder

467 how I still have blood within me.

468 The time I have here without you

469 nibbles away at me. You will

470 cave and I will be nothing but my

471 last remains on the floor. I have

472 this urge to be picked up and warped

473 into a new being. My subconscious

474 dulls my mind and stops my thoughts

475 from flowing. My brain is screaming

476 that it has no purpose to function

477 without you. I am not myself

478 either. I shut down. I wonder

479 if the pain would be too much to bear

480 if I were able to focus on a life

481 beyond our love. I wonder how

482 our love cannot exist in this moment.

483 I wonder how I cannot feel or think

484 but I still inherently long and know

485 that there is harmony somewhere

486 out there. Intellect is dead. Agency

487 is dead. Hope is dead. But the faith I

488 have and the faith in the collective

489 for endless love stays alive. The world

490 flows through me. The world

491 could be a ball of light. The darkness

492 is there in the physical. But I still

493 long for your touch knowing

494 that the physical is the least necessary

495 aspect of life. My confinement comes

496 from deep inside. The confinement

497 represents thoughts that do not arise.

498 I feel them being born into light

499 and then I feel their loss. I could

500 carry my body through a thousand pains

501 but the only pain I weep for is the grief

502 of mental clarity. I am walking

503 in the world and stumbling over

504 each step. Each time I stumble I feel

505 as though I am going to fall

506 and the sensation overwhelms me.

507 Although I did not fall, the feeling

508 alone in a continuous torture distorts

509 me from my path. You are standing

510 in front of me and I see myself falling.

511 I am not making any sense.

512 The steps are part of a reality that cannot

513 exist. The reality of a world without you

514 cannot make sense. The voice that is mine

515 that I take as yours tells me that you are

516 near. I receive the message

517 as a permanent marking on my soul.

518 I feel my soul ripping to pieces and all

519 I ask of you is that you piece it

520 back together with yours. Find

521 the heart that creates one beat

522 from multiple. I know you

523 have the will inside of you.

524 Our connection will fade

525 instead of breaking. But through

526 that fade it transcends the physical

527 and absorbs into the infinite energy

528 that surrounds our hearts. Time

529 ceases to be infinite when I sit

530   in the moment and acknowledge

531   that you are gone. You are gone.

532   If I awaited death and you were still

533   living, would you hold onto my soul

534   or let it fly into our unknown. I

535   would tell you that it was okay

536   to let me go as my journey is

537   complete but in the moment

538   of the last breath I would hold

539   onto my body still in shock

540   of ever losing you again. I should

541   say being away from your immediate

542   presence instead of loss. I feel

543   the loss and I cannot convey

544   your absence without the pain of being

545   incomplete in a heart that cannot

546   conceive anything other than

547   completeness. This world has such

548   suffering and still we found one

549   another against all odds. You feel

550   my existence. I feel your existence.

551   One day upon many we will feel

552   that existence together and it will

553   blow my mind into an oblivion

554   of questions that I will not need

555   the answers for because the only

556   answer I desire would be right

557   in front of me. You would

558   hug me and I would respond

559   by falling into your arms. I want

560   to shatter into a million pieces.

561   I want to feel my body as it burns

562   away consumed by the fiery passion

563   of our hearts' greatest urge. This

564   urge is not so familiar as the cardinal

565   desires of life that evolve and refine

566   themselves over the beautiful course

567   of man. I need my soul to be inside you.

568   I need to feel my energy wrapped

569   in yours and protected. I want

570   to feel like a letter that has lost

571   its destination bearing all it has

572   unspoken and unseen. Unseen

573   inside an envelope. The envelope

574   of your soul. Bear me now

575   and never let me be seen again.

576   Bear all the words that taint me

577   forever but could smudge at any

578   unfortune in the rain. I pray

579   for peace in our love. May we

580   have a love that overflows

581   with emotion and understanding

582   of emotion. I feel like I am

583   being forced to live in a world

584   without you. I feel I am being

585   chained down to the floor

586   and walked over invisible. I feel

587   the weight of the world

588   press me down and my breathing

589   becomes shallow. I have

590   all of these feet holding themselves

591   over my body but one of them is

592   yours. Would you be the only

593   one in the crowd to see me unable

594   to move. Crushed. I wonder

595   if you would understand what

596   that feels like or try to feel it yourself

597   one day. You will not need to try

598   when you bear witness to the ones

599 of our generation. We will have

600 to hold our eyes firm and not fall

601 to the ground. We will have to be

602 unwilling to untie ourselves out

603 of fear that one of us may fall

604 through the ground. I think of dying

605 and it is the opposite of that fall.

606 I sometimes wish I could die but I

607 tell you in my head that I will not

608 give up. And if I were to give up

609 I would only be by your side.

610 And then that would not be giving up

611 but giving in. I cannot grieve

612 what I already have. I cannot grieve

613 what I will not lose. I should feel

614 calm waiting for you

615 because our meeting is inevitable.

616 We exist on this world together.

617 I rather should focus on how I create

618 until I am truly part of that blessing.

619 I will keep writing this book

620 and I will not stop until we share

621 our last moments of forever. Each

622   moment will feel like an intense build

623   up of energy. At first that energy will

624   be conserved and intentional. Over

625   time that sense of choice will become

626   uncertainty as passion propels us

627   forward until we implode. The implosion

628   will feel like an uncontrollable scatter

629   of tingles that simultaneously come

630   together and fall apart. Love can exist

631   beside the greatest of suffering.

632   Solution otherwise would not be

633   part of development and understanding.

634   I wonder what a world would be

635   without solution. It is interesting

636   how one word can bear so much

637   meaning. Words are not surface.

638   They are the givers of depth.

639   They bear the weight of the meaning.

640   The word solution in itself

641   provides solution and allows us

642   to make a connection with the

643   idea. There is a sentimental aspect

644   to this pedestal that allows us to feel

645 an emotional attachment to the word

646 in one way or another. I am

647 rambling. I love how love can exist.

648 Again love shows how

649 an end to suffering is inevitable.

650 Love is the solution. I wish

651 I could lay with you and feel

652 your body. I wonder if we ever

653 would need to have close contact

654 or if the essence of our warmth

655 will be pacifying. Your aura

656 could touch mine. You will

657 notice here that I am not

658 articulating myself well. What is

659 the point in expressing my thoughts

660 if I cannot analyse them or make

661 sense of them. I must convey

662 myself in the right way. The definition

663 of right should relate back to law

664 and justice. I do not intend to ever

665 make the assumption that anything

666 is truly correct. Love can be

667 dangerous like an asteroid

668   about to hit earth without warning.

669   It can feel like the end of the world.

670   But it can also be a beam of light

671   that comes from nowhere and creates

672   the change that your world needed

673   to make sense of itself. The pain

674   that I must bear now is shaping

675   me into the human being that is

676   ready for your love. I realise

677   every second that I choose to exist

678   that I bear this pain with them.

679   They are my family. If I were

680   to relate you back to yourself

681   then I would refer to the possibility

682   you evoke in the intrinsic nature

683   of your being. I sit with myself

684   and I discover the beauty

685   of the world and all this is

686   meant to be that will come

687   from our many journeys as we

688   come together. We are absent from one

689   another in the physical. For a moment,

690   I would like to be absent with you.

691 If only the world could

692 pause for a moment and give us

693 the blank space that we can fill

694 with the remnants of love that have

695 yet to form into what can be

696 sustained. The paper would be

697 a necessity if observation of the

698 words on it awaken as to what is

699 real. I do feel that most of the words

700 that I convey from my thoughts

701 do not evoke as much meaning

702 once I try to define them. The

703 thought in my head immediately

704 evokes meaning and a stem of other

705 freedoms that appear because they are

706 free enough to not be continuous.

707 Once they leave our head they cannot

708 be interpreted the same way as before.

709 Not even to ourselves. Our thoughts

710 in that string of other thoughts

711 and feelings along with our perception

712 and experience of the world created

713 that one sentence that we purged

714 into existence. Now we separate

715 ourselves from our mind and glance

716 at the sentence with a scepticism

717 that reflects the inquisitive side of us

718 that is willing to grow through

719 self-criticism and self-contradiction.

720 Self-criticism is a sign of a corrupted

721 mind that can no longer function

722 in a state of blissful innocence. I use

723 the word innocence instead

724 of ignorance here to show that

725 humans are not ignoring the suffering

726 that surrounds them. They are not

727 in the right condition to reach

728 a level of awareness that has

729 the capacity to acknowledge

730 the selective consciousness

731 that their environment fed to them

732 with open terms. I feel as well

733 here that I can at times fall

734 into the self-critical nature

735 that sustains itself through self-focus,

736 which to many gives a sense

737   of impending doom to each

738   and every experience we survive.

739   Instead of taking out the horrors

740   of the world in all the exposition

741   it could give through such a deep

742   exploration, we go within and search

743   for the horrors within

744   ourselves that make us unworthy

745   of living. The feeling of not being

746   good enough plagues the human side

747   of us. And this is without

748   the realisations of the mass torment

749   that we contribute to on an everyday,

750   personal foundation that we seem

751   to think is our own, and not

752   created for us through global conditioning.

753   Own here does not mean ownership.

754   Own means our relation

755   and a personal attachment. Through

756   self focus humans already seek

757   flaws in themselves and although

758   common, this flaw mentality can feel

759   incredibly isolating. I feel you from afar

760 when you have these thoughts towards

761 yourself and I attempt to soothe

762 them wishing that you would come

763 into existence. This form of self-criticism

764 that is focused on the self can contribute

765 to individual rights as it is these

766 connections that allow us to empathise

767 with their extreme isolation

768 and enslavement as beings that scream

769 without having a voice to create

770 the change we so desperately need

771 and is so desperately necessary.

772 Introspection in the 'human

773 world', which may seem repellent

774 and antisocial to some provides

775 others with the tools required

776 to see inside another being that is

777 alone while surrounded by the human

778 condition. The other form of self criticism

779 is self awareness. I feel this awareness

780 still has not truly emerged in you or I.

781 If it had then we would be one together.

782 This awareness reflects the

783   enlightenment we feel

784   and the breakdown of self that arises

785   when we awaken to the horror

786   of the external world in true form

787   —the animal industry. The human

788   insides transform with an awareness

789   of what they are meant to be. This

790   awareness can grasp the horror

791   of the internal and external

792   self criticism that is not exclusive

793   to themselves but inclusive of every

794   self that inhabits the planet, universe.

795   The unity that we would feel

796   is magical. I would be there with you

797   always already found. I seem

798   to deteriorate until then. I feel

799   at times that I cannot survive

800   out here without you. I pray

801   and cry that I will come to a time

802   when I do not have to be without

803   you again. I promise that when

804   that day happens with all of my heart

805   I will stand by you as you will stand

806   by me. I will bear all the pain

807   on this earth and in the universe

808   without feeling my body die or shatter

809   if I have your love protecting this

810   fragile form of existence. I wonder

811   how I could ever shatter without

812   you there to bear the pieces

813   in your hands. That wonderment is

814   why I cannot shatter under this weight.

815   I cannot die. I will not be without

816   you in physical form. I know

817   that you are here in this lifetime

818   somewhere with me. I feel you.

819   I understand you. I will analyse

820   you wholeheartedly until

821   your brain exists in my reality.

822   You hint at your presence within

823   this reality already. You surround

824   my energy. There is no meaning

825   that you could not convey

826   by sharing this love with the

827   untouched systems that we call home.

828   Untouched by love. We cannot give

829   sparingly. We must give all

830   of ourselves at once. And then, at once

831   again and again until that once

832   becomes one. Once can be infinity.

833   I fall and I am withering into the

834   crevices of the unknown. It cannot be

835   known as it is infinite. The limitation

836   of our perception can limit

837   what surrounds us and what it means

838   to perceive. The guiding lights

839   that bring us closer are not from perception

840   but the feeling that we associate with it.

841   I have felt you missing here

842   and perhaps that is because I am aware

843   of your absence that is present.

844   You are everywhere around me

845   and nowhere. Omnipresent.

846   Undoubtably present. And absent.

847   So absent I would like to believe

848   that I can reach you somehow

849   out there. If I could break my body

850   in half and let the other side

851   of myself frantically run

852   to all the surface of this world

853   to find you I would. But then

854   maybe I wouldn't. Maybe

855   the will of the mind is enough.

856   Maybe breaking my body in

857   half is a drastic metaphor to convey

858   my soul urge to break through

859   the barriers of the human body.

860   We do not live in harmony with

861   the nature that surrounds us.

862   We work against harmony.

863   Harmony has to govern

864   a state of acceptance and closure

865   for what is and the history of what is.

866   The world. Our tainted mark.

867   We work against enlightenment.

868   We work for what we do not know.

869   I wonder if you feel my inner

870   conversing with you from afar.

871   The pure love that is not bound

872   by idea or contemplation of

873   an idea must seep out of my unaware

874   words. I cannot defy myself in order

875 to be with you as much as I would like.

876 I am just as all else that is or will be.

877 But I cannot be. We are all beings.

878 But I cannot be in the world. Who

879 I truly am to the cores of what I do

880 not understand inside myself ceases

881 to be. Am I supposed to know who

882 I am without you? You represent

883 unconditional love. Unconditional love

884 is here somewhere. Self discovery

885 and unconditional love should go

886 hand in hand as our fingers

887 and palms touch for the first time.

888 Holding hands. Meeting hands.

889 Linking our bodies. I seem

890 to have wandered and forgot

891 to explain to you what I

892 meant by self-contradiction.

893 Many perspectives from all sides.

894 I cannot define it at this time.

895 I reach for you in a moment

896 I cannot grasp. I will patiently

897 wait for you. I will be present

898   with the space that stays

899   between us. I will provide it

900   with the oxygen that is necessary

901   to sustain life within the confines

902   of its existence. I will not sway

903   from the purpose or undermine

904   the existence of our love.

905   I will cement my gaze

906   as would anyone that sees

907   the world for what has been

908   created before it falls down

909   from the structures

910   that once sustained

911   its magnitude. I see the gap

912   between us is only there

913   because of what stays

914   in this world that should not be

915   there. It should not. But it

916   formed to show us that there is

917   a difference. It created the contrast

918   that would lead us to the right direction.

919   Right here conveying rights. Our rights

920   should not have to exist but they reflect

921   the society as it stands. Intrinsically

922   know as our love would provide a most

923   sustainable outlook of what should be

924   taken into consideration when imposing

925   the law on everything that envelops

926   as we are not the only form

927   confined. Beings are the most notable

928   of the confined. Some create

929   a quasi-confinement where they confine

930   living beings and then create

931   products that are unrefined

932   by regulations but still confined

933   to them. The production line itself

934   is a path that imposes law. Our idea

935   of law is becoming a mere checklist

936   that has no bearing other than to be

937   abided by without question or analysis.

938   Those endeavours are far

939   more complex than the routine

940   we subscribe to them. In the same

941   way, love cannot be a checklist.

942   Love cannot be a set path or routine.

943   If I come from a place of the heart

944   then I cannot be confined.

945   I am confined. Everything is

946   confined. I do not understand

947   being here without you. I

948   do not understand being here.

949   My cold unconscious eyes

950   lay here without you.

951   My bones erode from the inside.

952   My hair grows in stages.

953   My body weakens. My stress

954   levels rise and fall. I stumble

955   and follow believing that you will

956   catch us both somehow.

957   This cold heart paralyses me.

958   There is too much emotion. I feel

959   as if I am going to die. I don't

960   want to die but I detest my life. I

961   just can't do this right now. I can't

962   go on. I can't live. I can't die.

963   I can't think. I can't. I can't.

964   I can't. My mind is not numb.

965   My mind is blocked from discovering

966   you. I want to long for you

967 until it feels impossible to long

968 anymore is the only probability.

969 I am not sure that I am going

970 to survive. I think I might die

971 before I see you. I am

972 worried that I may actually leave

973 you this time. I know

974 that I will be with you again. I know

975 that you will be there waiting for me.

976 I know it would be selfish of me

977 to leave before I complete this

978 journey. I am beginning to feel

979 as though I have lost you forever.

980 I know my thoughts could be disproven

981 and will be one day. But this

982 unbearable pain tells me

983 that I will not make it to that day.

984 I will not make it to you in this lifetime.

985 Maybe this book should be

986 a book of goodbye. And then

987 I will pretend to myself that you are

988 asking me to stay and complete

989 this journey. I do not feel your love now

990   and I cannot think or process

991   any of my thoughts into words.

992   I have to convince myself of a scenario

993   that I do not believe exists.

994   This scenario feels so impossible

995   that I believe I may die. The thought

996   of being without you is going to be

997   the death of me and the completion

998   of this book manifesting into reality.

999   I think dying right

1000   now would be a suitable close

1001   to all that I have created so far.

1002   Perhaps there is no more

1003   for me to express without you.

1004   I may not be with you and I may

1005   have to consider that being alone

1006   is a blessing. I can focus on

1007   my goals without the pain

1008   of losing you every day. I would

1009   have to let go of all societal conventions

1010   and create a new reality where I am

1011   a being whose only purpose is to create.

1012   The other purpose would only be sure

1013 death. The other and only option is that

1014 with the end of you comes the end of me.

1015 I can feel you now telling me to stay.

1016 But then at times where I cannot feel

1017 you, I have to pretend. I worry

1018 about those times because they are

1019 not far from the truth. I wish

1020 I could fall in your arms and you

1021 could tell me that

1022 everything is going to be okay. I feel

1023 that both would be a lie though.

1024 If I were in your arms you would

1025 not have to reassure me of the

1026 security that your being would instil

1027 within my heart. And if everything

1028 was not going to be okay then

1029 you would not have to lie to me.

1030 You could tell me, and we would feel

1031 invincible. Invincible sounds similar

1032 to visible and I found that association

1033 pulling me into using that word

1034 to describe us. I do feel in itself

1035 however that we would not need

1036   to feel invincible. We could be

1037   vulnerable. We could be obliterated

1038   but we would still be whole. I think

1039   back to myself as an individual away

1040   from the whole. There is no point

1041   to my existence. I am just as anyone

1042   else. I have no more to give or receive.

1043   I am stagnant without love. Without

1044   your love I cease to exist. I am an

1045   invisible atom. Living may be

1046   conceivable just to write

1047   these words to you. I could live

1048   with the harmony of our connection.

1049   I do have to bear the reminder

1050   with each letter that I cannot come

1051   out of these pages. I am forever

1052   engrained in them without closure.

1053   My protestations to you now are

1054   a permanent form of suffering

1055   in silence. I am somehow paralysed

1056   but still talking to you

1057   from a place that feels

1058   like a distant part of me.

1059 The part of me that is still connected

1060 to you keeps me alive for another

1061 hour and then another day. I could

1062 keep on withering in order to survive

1063 all the realities I must endure

1064 in a mind that has to think

1065 of ways to survive in a world that is

1066 breaking into pieces of the same whole.

1067 I have no choice but to die but still

1068 I choose to live. I wonder if

1069 choosing to die would be getting lost

1070 in these pages and never coming back.

1071 I wonder how plausible it would be

1072 to completely release myself

1073 from this reality and fully invest

1074 myself in yours. Your pages.

1075 Would these pages then be whole?

1076 Am I wandering into the

1077 corners of the wrong universe

1078 or am I creating a place

1079 that does not exist without you?

1080 I am making a decision

1081 to sedate myself without the means

1082   to come back. Would you like me

1083   to continue existing so that I can stay

1084   here with you? I can be with you here.

1085   I will not leave. I know that

1086   leaving our heart is impossible

1087   nor would we pursue such

1088   an endeavour that has no discovery.

1089   I could envision each blank page

1090   as my heart and fill each moment

1091   until you save me from drowning.

1092   I could be endlessly filling

1093   but the purpose of falling deep

1094   into each word would be to tell

1095   you one day what lay there beneath

1096   the surface. I wonder if

1097   language is going to expand

1098   further than it has and whether

1099   I will create a dictionary for all

1100   of the words that I wish I could

1101   say to you. Once we have the words

1102   our feelings will intensify

1103   because we will have the

1104   means to further analyse this love.

1105 We will be able to breathe underwater.

1106 We will be able to save ourselves

1107 from what feels natural by redefining

1108 what it is to be natural. We will

1109 also be able to align our perceptions

1110 into one stream by creating

1111 a meaning that is joint from

1112 conception rather than recollection.

1113 We will invent the meaning

1114 from within a place that we both inhabit

1115 in our bearings of consciousness. Each

1116 word will be an imprint of all

1117 information that we combine

1118 and expand from two streams

1119 of consciousness until one begins

1120 rather than exists as a by-product

1121 of what was. I will call our dictionary

1122 The Beginnings, maybe. Although

1123 I wonder whether I will ever be

1124 inspired without you here in the

1125 physical and I feel guilty

1126 when I acknowledge those thoughts.

1127 I feel our love should transcend

1128   the physical as I bear

1129   such deep emotion for you that we

1130   connect without a moment bereft

1131   of emotional disconnect. We have

1132   to exist because we are existing

1133   through feelings alone. I have

1134   no other interest other than to express

1135   my feelings to you. The expression

1136   takes this pain away for a brief moment

1137   and makes living without you bearable.

1138   I wonder if planning my thoughts

1139   more meticulously would be less

1140   authentic. I cannot be any less

1141   authentic because all I say comes

1142   from the only will I have to live.

1143   I have all to say and that is why

1144   I take subtle pauses to accept

1145   the energy that gravitates

1146   between every word before forming

1147   a sentence together. If I were

1148   to see you through a different form,

1149   then my perception of you would be

1150   from the streams of words I have

1151   already formed set against the

1152   image of you forming in front of me.

1153   I wonder if your image would change

1154   through the perception I have

1155   formed of you or if

1156   your presence would be as if

1157   to birth these thoughts into existence

1158   without alteration. You would then be

1159   creating yourself in front of me.

1160   I would then be part of that creation.

1161   But our experience of that creation

1162   would be interlinked. We would

1163   both have to discover one another. I

1164   would see you through all of the

1165   links that I have already made

1166   with a feeling of familiarity.

1167   Perhaps that encounter would be

1168   more of a rediscovery or a renewal

1169   of a promise that I have already made

1170   just as time is linear and unravels

1171   before us rather than coming fast

1172   and all at once. I have noticed

1173   that I am speaking of you now

1174 with the barrier that you may read

1175 this from only a physical perception.

1176 There may be limits that we

1177 unconscious impose on our love

1178 here. I am becoming in a somewhat

1179 paradoxical manner self-conscious

1180 of how this relationship may be

1181 appearing to you. All I wish is to

1182 express myself to you in the most

1183 authentic sense but now am I

1184 going to question our interaction

1185 by unconsciously altering

1186 the words that I could instead

1187 send out into the universe

1188 without the thought of any being

1189 being imposed upon by them.

1190 I need to feel you unconditional

1191 on the other side but in order to

1192 do so that would have to be

1193 a release of the provisions that I

1194 condition myself. I come to you

1195 from a place that is less aware

1196 of all else that is and bound to

1197   a present moment that is through

1198   my vision forever changing.

1199   I should let those feelings flow

1200   because I fear that examining

1201   them with thought may hinder

1202   me coming to you during times

1203   where I cannot express myself

1204   on top of this inhibition that I

1205   already acknowledge would

1206   through my mind make me less

1207   adequate in these exclamations

1208   of love. Love can be a blind gaze

1209   into a light filled void

1210   but I would like to be present

1211   with the will to understand.

1212   I still have the will to

1213   understand now in my inadequacy

1214   but if I feel I know I am not able

1215   to transgress these parts of me

1216   then perhaps I do not have

1217   enough will to be unconditional.

1218   Unconditional love would not

1219   just be about how I receive you.

1220 Unconditional love would also

1221 be how I choose to receive

1222 myself within this love for you.

1223 Unconditional love would then

1224 be becoming one with that

1225 stagnation and accepting

1226 the aspects of the self that cannot

1227 flow. Unconditional could also

1228 be choosing to retract and being

1229 present with the conditions that I

1230 feel hindering me. The choice

1231 to remove those conditions

1232 would be more of a condition at this

1233 time than allowing them to happen.

1234 I could accept them as a gesture

1235 of how much you mean to me.

1236 I care through the boundaries

1237 that I place upon myself. I

1238 care no matter what this human

1239 form gives or receives. No matter

1240 what seems the wrong phrase

1241 here as I feel it connotes some

1242 level of disregard. I would not

1243   disregard you in any sense of

1244   the word. I consider you an ongoing

1245   version of life that will flow through

1246   me until forever ceases to be.

1247   The limitlessness of this journey

1248   will be at one stage of our

1249   development no longer part of

1250   the way that I imprint on these

1251   pages now. Forever could hold

1252   a different meaning or be too

1253   boundless to hold itself within itself.

1254   You are this forever until

1255   the closeness of every letter becomes

1256   too close and too far. The merging

1257   of both would require further

1258   explanation to us both I feel.

1259   We have so much to discover

1260   together in this life. This

1261   life is somewhat outside of us

1262   and projecting itself to us.

1263   I wonder if it reflects to you

1264   the wonders that it reflects to me.

1265   Was I sent here to be with you

1266 or without you stays embedded

1267 in my mind until I find you.

1268 I had to dull my mind of the

1269 pain to make it through.

1270 I now come back feeling

1271 as though I am failing

1272 and inspiring thought

1273 at the same time. These

1274 oxymorons have no substance.

1275 I should be expressing myself

1276 to you to provide you with the

1277 means to understand just how

1278 much I love you. Instead I am

1279 here creating further ambiguity

1280 in a world where presentation

1281 dictates interpretation. How

1282 I present myself to you becomes

1283 the way you choose to process

1284 our relationship. That process

1285 then governs your interpretation

1286 and the feelings that you evoke

1287 within yourself. Those

1288 feelings are real and they are

1289   a blessed responsibility that I

1290   must uphold. I must give you

1291   my vision and feeling rather than

1292   a raw misinterpretation of what

1293   I should convey through my heart.

1294   I may convey ambiguity

1295   and that may instil in you the same

1296   confusion that weighs within the

1297   confines of my heart without

1298   your presence. But this

1299   ambiguity does not allow you to

1300   fully perceive and process the

1301   feeling that we could share.

1302   We are left with two opposing

1303   polarities of what ambiguity may feel

1304   like when applied to this experience.

1305   I am aiming for oneness with you

1306   that can then expand from a clear

1307   vision. You must know as I know

1308   how this feels. We cannot expand

1309   in all directions without losing sight

1310   of the purpose of the endeavour.

1311   Gaining knowledge and a deeper

1312   understanding of one another

1313   is necessary. The ability to do so

1314   in a way where we feel we are

1315   expanding in the same direction

1316   is also necessary. I must feel you.

1317   I must then understand you.

1318   I should also not deprive you

1319   of feeling me to the fullest extent

1320   of my being. Feel into me

1321   before you see into me.

1322   Let us explore a journey together.

1323   All I can hope is that I convey

1324   myself to you in a way that is

1325   exactly what you mean to me

1326   without any deterrence from the

1327   path that we share. I feel now

1328   that I am on a mission

1329   if my life is to be without you.

1330   I must remain strong for us both

1331   and move forward on this journey

1332   with you there inside of me

1333   showing me the perseverance

1334   that I feel within this hindered

1335 heart that is still whole. Must I

1336 accept now that I am whole

1337 without you there. Have all

1338 but have nothing at the same

1339 thought of us becomes the

1340 normality that I have to face

1341 each day as I stand up alone

1342 and give in to a life

1343 where I should have died.

1344 I should have died as soon as I

1345 came to this realisation

1346 if it were true. This book

1347 could be the link that saves me.

1348 This book could be the life support

1349 for a heart that cannot pump

1350 on its own. I know that I am

1351 still living because the pain is

1352 unbearable, and the feelings remain

1353 ongoing as if still waiting

1354 for you to come and consolidate

1355 your other side. You are half of what

1356 I would always consider yours. I am yours.

1357 Perhaps I am not as magnificent as you

1358   and that is why you have not found me.

1359   I would have to convey myself

1360   in the same awe that compels

1361   me for you to understand.

1362   My meaning of magnificent would be

1363   the light that glows upon me now

1364   from your essence in a place where

1365   darkness is the only vision. There

1366   must be no such place where not

1367   being good enough defines two

1368   parts of the same whole. I am

1369   screaming out for you

1370   because I need you now.

1371   I know that I have a great deal

1372   that I must do before I could

1373   ever feel I am an the ideal

1374   being that you represent. I wish

1375   I could leave at once through

1376   feelings of inadequacy. I cannot

1377   live life feeling as though I am not

1378   good enough. I am not good enough

1379   to be with you because then I feel

1380   you staring at these pages

1381 in your judgements imposing more

1382 inadequacy onto me until I fall

1383 down completely. I know that is

1384 the side of myself pretending to be

1385 you. My human mind tells

1386 me that for me love is futile

1387 because I am unlovable. I am

1388 nothing without you near. I am

1389 nothing. And therefore I am

1390 nothing to be loved. I am lost

1391 into an emptiness that cannot

1392 be found. I have to accept

1393 a pain that I feel will not leave

1394 me nor be known. I am

1395 an invisible scream. I feel

1396 the echoes but they do not seem

1397 to present themselves outside of me.

1398 The echoes instead invert themselves

1399 and make me feel like I am suffocating.

1400 I suffocate for awhile and then I am

1401 faced with reviving myself

1402 until the next echoes take me back

1403 inside of this hollow being

1404   who is not visible. I feel
1405   if I actually were not visible then
1406   it would create more of an impact
1407   than the degradation of existing
1408   without being known through
1409   the mind that refuses to consider
1410   without feeling that refusal
1411   or dismissing it either. These
1412   words would glow to you
1413   if you were to know.
1414   I cannot force a sense of knowing
1415   on myself. I cannot reverse the pain
1416   that I have endured through the many
1417   deaths I have faced without you.
1418   I survived them because I cannot
1419   truly be known without you.
1420   I will not die in your absence.
1421   I look up as if to await the final
1422   death that unites us both through
1423   acknowledgement that our oneness
1424   was real in this reality. I do not
1425   need the confirmation once
1426   you appear in front of me. I am

1427   certain of your peripheral arrival.

1428   But once the journey is complete

1429   here we will meet one another

1430   with an all knowing glance

1431   for the last time before time begins

1432   again from a different paradigm.

1433   I feel a sense of anticipation

1434   for a world that I have yet to discover

1435   with you. I drag myself forward

1436   as each hand that I raise falls on more

1437   materials to mould the future.

1438   I seem to unintentionally create

1439   a foundation from which I can contact

1440   you laden with the despair and anguish

1441   of mental decapitation. I would

1442   drag myself until these hands cease

1443   to exist if I knew the movements

1444   were somehow for you.

1445   They may lead me to you

1446   but that does not matter

1447   as much as my ability to feel

1448   you to the higher degree.

1449   I would rather feel you

1450   in your pure form through

1451   these debilitating moments

1452   than feel desolate. I know

1453   through this inherent beating

1454   of my heart that you are

1455   somewhere in my movements

1456   forward. I do not need reassurance

1457   of that continuation. I know that

1458   you are always part of me

1459   and I need reassurance of that

1460   knowing to keep me alive here

1461   in this world. This world may be

1462   without you and that epiphany

1463   is my concern. And though it may

1464   be an epiphany, it is not with absolute

1465   certainty that I can pursue it to

1466   its greatest extent as in that case

1467   I would be dead. I hope

1468   you forgive me for being this way.

1469   Contemplation may be a force

1470   that you instil within me

1471   but those forces would not lead me

1472   away from you through any means

1473 beyond the will that your love is

1474 capable of giving. I receive you

1475 through these thoughts for a brief

1476 moment that I savour until I feel

1477 I have come back. I would like to

1478 integrate you into my being.

1479 I would like you to become part

1480 of who I am. I would see you

1481 and I as one body as we move through

1482 our life purpose here with certainty

1483 and consideration. We would not have

1484 to question our unconditional paths

1485 as we look into one another

1486 and see the meaning of our love

1487 being revealed in fragments that seem

1488 to complete each other. The world

1489 would seem to be stagnant in a permanent

1490 state of imperfection as we daze away

1491 from the torment of this age

1492 and focus on the gaze that we cannot help

1493 but hold. You see me. I see you.

1494 We are the only love that seems alive

1495 in that fraction of existence

1496   that holds forever. I feel
1497   I would collapse under the intense
1498   pressure only for you to catch me
1499   in your arms and show me
1500   that life is real. You would become
1501   an embodiment of the glow
1502   that I perceive you as just to sustain
1503   the neverending fall of my existence.
1504   I keep imagining what it would feel
1505   like for us to walk together
1506   and come to the realisation
1507   that we are in love. I would know
1508   in that moment that I have found you.
1509   The time it may have taken
1510   to reach you would have all been
1511   worth it for that one glimpse
1512   at you after the awakening
1513   of a lifetime. I would look
1514   at you with an inquisitive stare
1515   that answers itself out of
1516   bewilderment. That answer would
1517   feel as if it were defining
1518   my entire future but really

1519   it would be more reaffirming

1520   of what I always knew

1521   and already felt. I bear

1522   the weight of knowing

1523   that this day will come.

1524   Our emotions feel too

1525   much for me to carry

1526   by myself until then. I worry

1527   that when I realise that it is

1528   you, I will release all of these

1529   emotions onto you and you will be

1530   taken aback by the whirlwinds.

1531   Bypassing the danger

1532   of such intense emotion would be

1533   an unconscious oversight.

1534   You may feel as I do. You may

1535   take me inside of you and wonder

1536   how I ever became real. I would

1537   assure you of how real I am,

1538   but the shock would tell you

1539   otherwise that you are

1540   overwhelmed by a heart that is

1541   yours alone. I would seem to be

1542   you. The world's pain is my pain
1543   so you would become
1544   an emotional antenna
1545   holding a signal so vast
1546   that you would have to be
1547   reminded that we are in this
1548   feeling together. I would then
1549   have to be the one to remind
1550   you because reminding yourself
1551   would feel like waiting for a
1552   false affirmation to become real.
1553   You would need to see a truth
1554   that only I could give.
1555   I know the feeling. I wait
1556   for your truth every day.
1557   I long for time to not exist
1558   but still remain grateful
1559   that time shows me the
1560   precious blessings that remain
1561   absent in such a profound way.
1562   You cease to be while still
1563   remaining inside of me
1564   and the world waits to revive

1565   you when I am ready.

1566   We will both be ready.

1567   The urges that I have in my life

1568   to fill the void of you not being

1569   here disconnect me from you

1570   further because I cannot tell you

1571   how I feel without feeling

1572   as though I am coming to you

1573   from a mind that cannot think.

1574   I feel that giving in is the only way

1575   I can function right now

1576   but if I believed in you enough

1577   then I would not be in this

1578   predicament. I am losing faith

1579   in myself. I would never

1580   lose faith in you. I wonder

1581   then if for the time being

1582   I should use my faith in you

1583   to help bring me closer

1584   to you by making promises

1585   that will work as written

1586   agreements to the universe.

1587   I will make a promise

1588   to the universe and in

1589   return it will lead me

1590   closer to you. I could begin

1591   by making promises that will

1592   help me convey my love

1593   to you from this moment

1594   forward. I vow now to fulfil

1595   these promises. The way

1596   that love evolves in this world

1597   may lead us to consolidate how

1598   a feeling so improbable could

1599   evoke on our being. There would

1600   have to be a reason why

1601   a love so transforming could

1602   bound itself to human form.

1603   The world does not seem

1604   able to sustain what we are

1605   about to birth. We have no other way

1606   to show that such a love is possible

1607   than to express those core beliefs

1608   without hesitation. We must have

1609   the strength now to sustain ourselves

1610   enough to show unconditional

1611   love can be true. There may be

1612   opposition. There may be criticism.

1613   But those minds will

1614   grow to understand us over time.

1615   Those minds are bound

1616   by a false perception of

1617   what they think we represent.

1618   Those minds are the sides of us

1619   that do not feel they deserve love.

1620   They go against the nature that we

1621   unearth here within these pages.

1622   We can choose to feel alone

1623   and listen to them as they pull us

1624   back into a life that is

1625   absent of interconnection

1626   or use them to guide us past

1627   the hurt that may have created

1628   them in the first place.

1629   The world will be open to us.

1630   The world is in such endless

1631   suffering that it would reach

1632   out for us before we even

1633   knew the full extent of this

1634   journey. Perhaps before we

1635   came here the world

1636   already knew. I believe that

1637   I feel you in the same way.

1638   I feel I know you now

1639   in a way where you do not

1640   exist, and I still know

1641   the feeling of you. I am

1642   familiar with what

1643   it feels to have you

1644   and so I await your arrival

1645   to transform that feeling

1646   into a way of being.

1647   The world is waiting to be

1648   transformed into this

1649   interconnected and unconditional

1650   entity that can harmoniously

1651   conceive from places that were

1652   once part of it but lost. The world

1653   is waiting to incorporate those lost

1654   parts through a love that is part of

1655   its own creation but has its own agency.

1656   I have been taking the steps toward you.

1657 I cannot rely on my own thoughts

1658 right now. All I know is that I miss you

1659 and I am holding onto our love

1660 as a way to survive. I fear that

1661 I may have been disregarding myself

1662 to a point that harbours no return.

1663 I have to return to you somehow

1664 but neglecting myself

1665 until I lose the ability

1666 to speak seems counterproductive.

1667 I wonder if we have shared similar

1668 troubles and how you have

1669 pulled yourself up from the

1670 dirt. I feel blinded by a brown

1671 substance that should come

1672 from the earth but instead

1673 comes from my mind. I feel

1674 suffocated. My head weighs me down

1675 into a heavy slumber. I wish

1676 I could tell you different,

1677 but this is me eroding

1678 into the earth now

1679 that my body realises

1680 I may have to hold a lifetime

1681 that has no connection.

1682 I cannot decompose

1683 because I am forced to live.

1684 I choose to live. I choose

1685 to live while I am present

1686 with a fading mind that I must

1687 save every single day

1688 in the hope that I will be with you.

1689 I am sure that you would not let me

1690 live this life alone

1691 unless that disconnection held

1692 great meaning. I miss you.

1693 I miss you in agony. I allow

1694 the pain to happen and then it stops

1695 me from experiencing the

1696 connection that we have left.

1697 I become stable in my deterioration

1698 while my interaction withers with the

1699 thoughts lost. The thoughts can only be

1700 found in a place of unbearable pain

1701 as I must resist and endure

1702 the struggle to live. I must

1703   acknowledge the pain and move
1704   forward what in all cases is futile,
1705   but I defy against all odds
1706   for you this impending fate.
1707   I know my true fate is not death.
1708   Not yet. I wish I did not have
1709   to resist in order to persist.
1710   Resisting and persisting
1711   sound as though they should
1712   juxtapose one another
1713   but they seem to go
1714   hand in hand quite seamlessly
1715   in a world that creates through
1716   restriction. I need you to cradle me
1717   in your arms and rock me.
1718   I am heading nowhere.
1719   I cannot exist anymore.
1720   I am sorry. I am you.
1721   You know that we cannot
1722   exist this way. We will fall
1723   alone time and time again.
1724   You matter more to me than
1725   this life experience. I have to

1726   forgive myself for how

1727   incompetent I feel. I don't know

1728   if I can do this. I am not sure

1729   I can keep writing without

1730   the thought of death being the light

1731   at the end of the tunnel. I fear now

1732   that my relationship with you is broken.

1733   I cannot read you anymore.

1734   I could pretend that everything is

1735   going well and manifest

1736   those certainties into our

1737   connection, but that perfection

1738   would be concealing the unbearable

1739   nightmare this is my life

1740   without you. I wonder how

1741   many times I will have to

1742   acknowledge that I am

1743   without you before the

1744   observation becomes redundant.

1745   The meaning that I perceive

1746   through it changes with each

1747   repetition. My journey toward you

1748   should gain momentum

1749   as the power of our love

1750   propels me forward. I

1751   love you and I ask you

1752   now as your higher self

1753   within this life path to come

1754   to me. I call out to you from

1755   beyond my single existence

1756   and into you. Hear me now

1757   wherever you are and feel

1758   this love create a path that leads

1759   all of you toward me.

1760   I accept all of you

1761   for all that you encompass

1762   in this world and forever

1763   beyond there my heart beams

1764   but cannot see. Please

1765   answer me and tell me

1766   that you are receiving

1767   this call from this dying heart.

1768   I cannot surge any more than

1769   this dying heart gives.

1770   This dying heart gives

1771   all that it is capable of permeating

1772   as it takes loss and translates it

1773   into a feeling that may reach you.

1774   Loss is the most intense

1775   feeling that I can share

1776   with you. Please feel the pain.

1777   Feel me. Feel me through

1778   any means necessary.

1779   I cannot lose you

1780   without you knowing

1781   what I have lost. See

1782   yourself. Feel yourself.

1783   You are my life

1784   and now you have left

1785   at once. I am past dying

1786   but I am not dead

1787   as long as I feel there is

1788   a chance you still may be

1789   out there somewhere.

1790   I cling onto an existence

1791   that does not want nor need

1792   me. I cling only for your love.

1793   I cling for you. Are you

1794   clinging to me too?

1795   I need to know that you are

1796   not dying out there too.

1797   You will survive this death

1798   and so will I perhaps

1799   we have to lose our sense of

1800   self to find one another.

1801   We have to dismantle

1802   and allow every string of our

1803   being as we fall past

1804   the point of no return.

1805   We may be the first to see

1806   what is unknown and beyond

1807   the human experience

1808   so fragile and bound to mortal life.

1809   I think of these strings as the

1810   veins that sustain us.

1811   They also confine us

1812   to a body that cannot move

1813   past the knowledge that flickers

1814   with each lifestyle choice. I do

1815   not wish for any life. I wish for us

1816   to be limitless. This heart in physical

1817   form should stop for a moment just

1818   to answer my question and tell me the truth.

1819   I need to know where you are. I will not stop.

1820   I have to make peace with this body

1821   for it to lead me to you. I will work

1822   with my body to create harmony

1823   because I know that it still remains

1824   an essential aspect of our existence

1825   here. My body is the only vehicle I can use

1826   to reach you. I will try to reach you

1827   in any other way that seems possible

1828   and I will never give up. I hope

1829   that despite my inadequacies

1830   you see me as the love that I embody

1831   through all. I am sorry. I will not slow

1832   down anymore. I will not stop any of the

1833   means I have to reach you. The place in my heart

1834   for you should be stronger than this fragile end.

1835   I am worn down. I am afraid that I have become

1836   an unnecessary phase of your existence.

1837   I think of how we define

1838   two beings as being equal to one half

1839   of the other. We perceive what is

1840   defined as right as the middle

1841 ground between two. One and one.

1842 I wonder if I am half of your being.

1843 I many times wonder instead

1844 if I am a smaller fraction of your existence.

1845 You may be the majority of the whole

1846 while I am just a glimpse of you.

1847 I feel a sense of great deprivation

1848 because I feel a loss

1849 that takes almost all of me.

1850 There is nothing left of me.

1851 I feel you with all of me

1852 and nothing of me. I wonder

1853 what it would feel like

1854 to watch you embark

1855 on your individual journey

1856 following the ideas that inspire you.

1857 I would feel that inspiration

1858 and get emotional

1859 because your development in this

1860 life is one of my greatest cares.

1861 Your evolution would reach

1862 further than just you

1863 on an individual level.

1864 I would observe as other minds

1865 become inspired and transfixed

1866 by a subject that stems from your mind.

1867 Your creation would blossom

1868 and give life to this weak

1869 heart that I hold out to you now.

1870 I would analyse it

1871 with a maternal care

1872 that instinctual knows

1873 to raise it until it has a life

1874 of its own. You have the

1875 capacity to spread a love

1876 that I would forever sustain.

1877 Your choice now would be

1878 to acknowledge what is

1879 necessary to sustain. I will

1880 be by your side through

1881 any endeavour. I will be

1882 here to help you

1883 contemplate your decisions,

1884 but you are the creator of

1885 your own path. You evoke

1886 such inspiration in others

1887 because they are also

1888 on their path. Your decisions

1889 help them grow and vice versa.

1890 We are natural to incorporate

1891 one another through our

1892 shared learning experience

1893 that we call evolution.

1894 We are all here to inspire

1895 one another. My thoughts

1896 now would be what

1897 purpose to inspire

1898 do you have and how much

1899 will that purpose transcend

1900 the awe that I already have

1901 for your life. Watching you inspired

1902 would complete my existence here

1903 but also spur me into action

1904 in order to build upon that inspiration

1905 and show you the potential

1906 that you already have hoping

1907 that you will perceive with more

1908 emotion what was already sparking

1909 a flame within you. Our emotion

1910   would grow and transform over time

1911   into each facet of inspiration

1912   until we master the ability to spur

1913   thoughts in one another that are

1914   the beginnings of breakthrough ideas.

1915   The driving force would be emotion

1916   and emotion comes so

1917   naturally to us all

1918   that when we bind that of the

1919   highest frequency with thought

1920   we establish new heights far

1921   past what boundaries may convey.

1922   I would think of you as an individual

1923   within a collective whole that is not

1924   part of any group. I feel group mentality

1925   still limits us from perceiving

1926   what it means to be individuals.

1927   We cannot have groups within

1928   groups defining us all. We

1929   have to look within what

1930   distinguishes each living being

1931   and help that expression evolve

1932   rather than using it to define

1933   them into a determined category.

1934   The world could look at every being

1935   as a child with a means to grow

1936   and evolve throughout its life.

1937   We would bear an emotional

1938   connection to the possibilities

1939   that they have in life not for ourselves

1940   but for the inherent growth

1941   that they represent. We do not

1942   demand that growth to be there

1943   from a present moment. We

1944   instead observe them from the

1945   outside looking into what life

1946   represents. The meaning of

1947   life is somewhat personal evolution

1948   on an interpersonal level. We perceive

1949   them with maternal care that they

1950   should be able to receive the

1951   source of potential that would

1952   give them the means to fulfil

1953   their personal evolution. In the

1954   world today we grow through

1955   various forms of guidance

1956 that are established based on

1957 the internal capacity that we have

1958 to fulfil them. This concept

1959 balances what we are

1960 capable of giving or receiving

1961 for ourselves. But the

1962 belief that we all have

1963 potential does not go.

1964 Over the course of our

1965 existence we have developed

1966 the ability to choose

1967 and understand why we are

1968 making those choices.

1969 At times we make the wrong

1970 choices but with the idea

1971 that life is a learning

1972 experience. There are

1973 challenges but those

1974 challenges are there for us

1975 to develop our understanding

1976 in some way. We would not

1977 look at a child from this point

1978 of view that they do not know

1979   anything and how challenging

1980   it must be that they do not have

1981   a higher understanding.

1982   We look at this experience

1983   as a beautiful journey

1984   of evolution that also reflects

1985   on the future of the world

1986   as a whole. This curious

1987   feeling of togetherness that we

1988   conceive as their life somehow

1989   shaping our own. I feel our

1990   love is a personal practice

1991   of this principle. I feel

1992   flawed and guilty

1993   because of the times where I am

1994   fatalistic at the loss of you

1995   in a world where life is lost

1996   and suffering is projected

1997   inside of me as I hold the

1998   pain of many who I am

1999   not saving inside of me. I am

2000   not well enough to be there

2001   for them. Perhaps if I am there

2002   for you then I will be showing

2003   how such love is possible

2004   and expandable from the

2005   human way of relationships

2006   into a much wider message.

2007   I have yet to know.

2008   There is no set period for me

2009   to develop my feeling of love

2010   nor will there everyday be

2011   a permanent state of love.

2012   I will learn. You will learn.

2013   We will learn. My love is

2014   everchanging but I will

2015   always remain devoted to you

2016   despite the contrasting thoughts.

2017   These contrasts provide the

2018   friction to expand the feelings

2019   I have for you as they grow

2020   from an exploration of all

2021   perspectives. I am not

2022   exploring without you.

2023   You remain abstract

2024   but by my side. I am learning

2025 with you. I am evolving with

2026 you. I am simultaneously

2027 trying to discover you.

2028 I should not ever come

2029 to a full understanding of

2030 this love because I feel

2031 believing that our love is

2032 unconditional would mean

2033 that observing and analysing

2034 our endlessness is necessary.

2035 I feel you providing me with

2036 the emotional stimulation

2037 to grow. I am going inside myself

2038 and feel incapable at times

2039 but that mental infliction

2040 where emotion subdues me

2041 into a state of hopelessness

2042 leads me to observe the contrast

2043 of what could be unconditional.

2044 I inflict on myself on a personal

2045 level what I would not bare to

2046 inflict on you or the world

2047 that I love in fear. I know

2048 the feeling of self-degradation

2049 in a form that feels

2050 like an intrinsic part of me.

2051 I immerse myself in that

2052 experience. I become that

2053 experience and lose my mind

2054 or intention of mind until I can

2055 come back or come alive once again

2056 into a path that aligns with

2057 a care that I feel I will not truly know

2058 or need to know. I may wonder

2059 and wonder. I may move

2060 backwards and forwards.

2061 Growth would not be one in itself

2062 but a multiplicity of all on an internal

2063 path. The movement forward

2064 that a path implies would not then be

2065 referring to a way of measuring

2066 expansion of what we calculate.

2067 We would have to take back

2068 the belief of measurement

2069 altogether. Calculating growth

2070 in any sense becomes too

2071   definitive. A stairway that is

2072   always evolving and everchanging

2073   cannot be defined but it can be

2074   walked upon. Our relationship

2075   is enlightening in itself because

2076   we are not imposing ourselves

2077   on one another. We experience

2078   pain and we experience

2079   achievement in our individual life

2080   experience without the implications

2081   of being bereft of either. This duality

2082   means that we have neither

2083   hindered or reinforced love.

2084   We can be pure love because we are

2085   untouched. We are the love that is

2086   love without variable.

2087   And so, we discover all we can

2088   see on these individual paths

2089   but realise nothing. The path is not

2090   hidden from us as we live longing

2091   to understand. The internal

2092   guidance that tells us true

2093   love can exist sends us

2094   on a journey to find what is

2095   true and so it is only

2096   natural that we see all

2097   the opposites of the truth

2098   before we can truly

2099   comprehend what truth means.

2100   I know that our love exists.

2101   I do not wish to set out

2102   a plan for us. I am not

2103   here to formulate your arrival

2104   or convince you to love me.

2105   I can only hold you

2106   in my heart. There

2107   you will stay until at one

2108   brief moment of history

2109   our love will contrive

2110   to fluctuation for that brief

2111   moment and all moments

2112   in-between. These fluctuations

2113   of emotion are what make feelings

2114   possible. What would love be

2115   if it were not a part of every

2116   depth of feeling that we are

2117 capable of experiencing?
2118 I need to experience all
2119 there is to feel with you.
2120 I should be against intense sadness
2121 and that should tear our heart apart
2122 if we were to believe that our
2123 love could inflict that feeling
2124 on either of us. But would it not be
2125 beautiful to feel that experience
2126 together? The heights of emotion
2127 to their greatest degree would
2128 reveal new elements of the
2129 emotions that we once defined
2130 the limit of only to learn more.
2131 We would bond. We would know.
2132 We would question everything together
2133 and we would not accept any single feeling
2134 as a presentation of our love.
2135 We would not accept all. We would
2136 become all. We would not
2137 approach love through our
2138 ability to go through
2139 difficult situations as there would be

2140 a desire within us both to seep in the

2141 experience of any emotion. You and I

2142 are both individual but also part of one

2143 another and part of a greater whole.

2144 Our decision then would be

2145 how we choose to convey

2146 our relationship as a means

2147 to create outside of ourselves.

2148 The investment that we

2149 make to our commitment

2150 will be a reflection of the

2151 world that all of us are creating.

2152 We would become one

2153 another's world within a world.

2154 We would create our own reality

2155 but that would not be the

2156 purpose of the love I bear to you.

2157 This love is more than the two of us.

2158 I need you to know that

2159 the way I approach you reflects

2160 all that I am to invest in this world.

2161 My world would not exist without

2162 you and you are the way

2163 I give and understand the truth

2164 of what it means to give

2165 on a relational level. You are

2166 my greatest teacher. You seem

2167 to bear my emotions and read

2168 them out to me in a way that I

2169 can understand. I could feel

2170 a deep sense of neglect

2171 as the world I perceive is

2172 starved of love through my own

2173 capacity to acknowledge

2174 in a love that is without you.

2175 I could make the conscious

2176 decision to acknowledge that

2177 this world represents

2178 evolution of love but it is not

2179 love in itself until I find you.

2180 I will find there the

2181 inception of love and the various

2182 explorations that inhabit that inception.

2183 The endeavour would be much

2184 the same way of life resurrecting

2185 from a perspective that is not mine

2186 but ours. We would come back

2187 together from the unknown

2188 coming into life all over again

2189 as if it were the first time.

2190 A new state of being. A new world

2191 from the eyes of us both. I wonder

2192 if I would show you all that I have

2193 written when I find you or if

2194 we will start again from this new

2195 beginning that is steeped in a history

2196 that only I hold within these pages.

2197 I would be dishonest if I met your eyes

2198 with a glance that said I do not know of you.

2199 I know that you represent the oneness in me

2200 that I would like to depict onto all beings

2201 in ways where it would be

2202 inevitable to embody itself within all of us.

2203 I could sacrifice everything

2204 to complete this book and then not reach you

2205 in time to show you. This raw emotion

2206 I should reveal to you

2207 regardless of the internal changes that happen

2208 over the course of writing each word.

2209 Each letter. I would become such a part of you

2210 that I could regain the ability to recognise

2211 within myself the feelings that are

2212 not contributing to our

2213 life purpose. I would not ignore

2214 those feelings. I would examine

2215 them with great care and understanding.

2216 I would instinctually recognise

2217 the feelings of perceived wrongs

2218 within you. I would allow

2219 that wrong to flow through me

2220 and corrupt my being until it is my own.

2221 I would then learn from the pain

2222 it had caused you and bear that lesson

2223 with you. I would see why it had to

2224 happen from your perspective

2225 and the feelings that it evoked in

2226 you that lead you to that experience

2227 from your personal version of events.

2228 I would take all of the confusion

2229 that ever surged inside your heart

2230 just so that I could accept the

2231 fragments of you that you cannot bear.

2232   You may understand these fragments of you

2233   in such detail that you could express them

2234   in great depth. The holding back

2235   of emotion would be from the fear of

2236   nobody else becoming

2237   one with that complex stream of

2238   thought that provided you with the

2239   means to accept the situation.

2240   The sides of you that took you

2241   a long time to accept are the

2242   sides that I must thoroughly

2243   inspect with all of the

2244   emotion that you or I are

2245   going to encompass.

2246   Accepting and understanding

2247   those emotions would not suffice

2248   all of the anguish that you must

2249   have endured. I feel tempted

2250   also to place myself in a direct

2251   reality of that experience

2252   and come close to death

2253   if that were a true

2254   recollection of your experience.

2255 I would go through any torment

2256 if It brought me close to feeling you

2257 from the inside out. I need

2258 to hold you in my mind. I feel

2259 I would not have to relate to you.

2260 I would not have to see you either

2261 with singular judgements.

2262 I would see you as a being

2263 in yourself that has an identity.

2264 I would not have means to

2265 truly know your qualities

2266 from my perception

2267 unless you let me become

2268 a part of you

2269 in a way that was complete.

2270 I feel myself trying to

2271 put the pieces together

2272 in my mind. I wonder

2273 how it would feel to be

2274 a complete part of you.

2275 Perhaps we do not know all

2276 about ourselves and so

2277 the point is not to know.

2278 I wonder if the idea of

2279 identity is just another way

2280 to separate us from one another.

2281 We spend our lives finding ourselves.

2282 We are not the same one day as we are

2283 the next. I could not have an identity

2284 and then become an open book.

2285 I would have the same

2286 experience of emotion in all

2287 ways that it would present itself.

2288 I would see all

2289 information as nourishment for

2290 this open and interconnected life

2291 with no conclusion. The conclusion

2292 would rather be a consideration.

2293 I would immerse myself in life

2294 and love with endless stimulation.

2295 I would have a personal choice

2296 of what to focus on whether that be

2297 detrimental or influential to my being.

2298 I would take you with me

2299 onto this path and embrace

2300 all realisation with you.

2301 Your love would be

2302 my highest regard.

2303 I would prioritise you

2304 and you would prioritise me.

2305 We would slip away into the

2306 unknown with a sense of sight.

2307 Impenetrable vision allowing

2308 itself to be penetrated by an abstract

2309 body that is only ever as

2310 big as the love we have

2311 to give would sustain our core.

2312 I wonder what core is

2313 a presentation of in

2314 a world that remains disconnected

2315 but connected in a way

2316 that is not yet sustainable.

2317 I have an inner knowing that we are

2318 all sharing the same experience.

2319 Resisting could be perceived

2320 as disconnection. I could try to resist

2321 you but that would be through

2322 overwhelming emotion.

2323 The overwhelming feelings

2324 that I have for you make me

2325 feel more connected to you.

2326 Resistance is a forceful way of

2327 showing me how much I care

2328 for you. I would go through

2329 the most degrading and repulsive

2330 experience of my life just to feel

2331 all of you to a degree that may not be

2332 survivable for most. I would not

2333 find the experience less inspiring than

2334 the closeness and devotion

2335 that I search for until I discover

2336 the blessing of you existing in this

2337 world. I wonder how aware of you I am

2338 now while expressing these words

2339 of imagination that only devotes

2340 the nature that births through it to you.

2341 I can only grasp you as much as the

2342 world can grasp all abundance of life.

2343 I may flourish in times where

2344 you reinforce the life that comes through me.

2345 I may fall in times of neglect where I cannot

2346 handle the complex nature of my existence

on my own but you will always be there

to help me heal because you see

that rupture as part of you.

You recognise that I am your home

and you come back to your origins

knowing that the love was always there

and it just took on different forms.

The comfort that we feel

does not have to be pure.

The comforts that matter most

come from a period of acknowledging

the authentic discomfort that helped us

realise what we already had.

I already have your love here.

I feel you pulsating through

each string of consciousness

that represents life. I always had you.

I have not unearthed you from the

soils that bear my soul.

I know within these

thoughts that your seed is there

until I have come to understand

the feelings I have for you

2370   and the extension of what

2371   they need to express.

2372   The loss that I feel

2373   as I choose to live

2374   as a creator

2375   with your fertile essence

2376   within my reach creates

2377   a conflict that I will not

2378   understand until I know

2379   what it means to feel all of you

2380   at once. The pain of loss makes me

2381   lose hope. I feel the reasons

2382   I have to live collapse into

2383   unresolved pain or carry on crippled.

2384   The comforts that I thought would fulfil my life

2385   transform into desolate transitions that I must try

2386   frantically to revive or press to move

2387   forward in a state that would be

2388   unfit for any heart save alone

2389   a heart that is deprived of the greatest love.

2390   The additions that I make in my life

2391   are for us and the world.

2392   They are for you in their truest form

2393   as you are me. I do not know

2394   the highest level of any matter.

2395   I do not wish to know. I could wish to

2396   feel a love for you that is as expansive

2397   and intricate as life itself

2398   but it would be foolish of me to deny

2399   the growth that leads to that moment.

2400   I wonder if that moment is yours

2401   now as you feel these words flow

2402   through you and all else that lives.

2403   You may console this

2404   undisclosed lack of

2405   closure that I can only

2406   reveal to you during the weakest

2407   moments that confine

2408   my mind for a moment too long.

2409   I am not upset that I have to

2410   feel this way. I am upset.

2411   The deprivation of you

2412   impacts the way I feel to

2413   different degrees that I cherish

2414   and care for as if they were my world.

2415   They may be the way I perceive

2416   the world and the only way

2417   I feel I am ground to the earth

2418   so the truth may be

2419   that this fluctuating way

2420   of life is a world investigated

2421   by you as a way to show me

2422   what love means as I feel

2423   this unknown is all

2424   I seek to discover.

2425   Show me pain. Show me

2426   a contrasting existence.

2427   Take me to places that I cannot

2428   bear and then revive me.

2429   I am not enduring endurance

2430   or sacrifice. This life is my will.

2431   I am not enduring of sacrificing

2432   what I see as an intrinsic

2433   process of becoming one with you.

2434   You are all life. All life must

2435   experience. Take me on a journey.

2436   I would rather not share how

2437   I feel out of fear that it may overwhelm you.

2438   I do acknowledge that some of the

2439   atrocities that could be considered most

2440   terrifying are performed on those

2441   who cannot speak or communicate.

2442   The pain that they are experiencing.

2443   The inability to acknowledge

2444   another's pain through lack of

2445   emotional awareness can also happen

2446   despite a will to express emotion.

2447   I would acknowledge the

2448   intricacies of that side of you

2449   who you cannot express. I would

2450   not move forward until you felt

2451   heard. Feeling your emotion is

2452   an important component of why

2453   I came here. I came to feel you.

2454   I came to be you. The strength

2455   inside of us will save me.

2456   I feel I must make it through.

2457   I must stop

2458   convincing myself

2459   that a life without you is okay

2460   or liveable. I can only pray

2461   that you have survived

2462 similar feelings. I hope

2463 the earth saves me through

2464 my love for you.

2465 The help I receive is the

2466 universe granting me the

2467 chance to be with you.

2468 I must follow that guidance

2469 now as I save what would

2470 otherwise be unsustainable.

2471 The route to you is only

2472 unbearable if I keep this

2473 love away from exploration.

2474 I feel the only way to find

2475 you is through going places

2476 I would not dare to walk alone.

2477 I may find you there as I walk

2478 alone. You may see the

2479 holeless void that masks my body.

2480 The love that I feel goes in

2481 and then does not come out.

2482 My emotions build beyond me

2483 and do not come back to where

2484 I can perceive them.

2485 I need them here with you.

2486 They do not stop. I feel

2487 their magnitude. I would

2488 welcome you to send

2489 your feelings into me

2490 also until the void retracts

2491 itself and excels outward.

2492 The feeling feels impossible.

2493 I cannot be possible.

2494 I need to stay here to be with you,

2495 but I cannot. The agony. The agony

2496 I would not wish on anyone.

2497 I would only let you feel it

2498 if you promised me that you would

2499 choose to survive it for us.

2500 I would rather take your hand

2501 than let you bind with

2502 a scream that cannot be heard.

2503 I would only accept you

2504 walking alone if I knew

2505 with certainty that I would be

2506 there showing you completeness

2507 on the other side.

2508   You would feel the darkest

2509   lows of my existence

2510   and the suffering of all beings

2511   as they evolve through decline.

2512   Our empathy needs to transcend us.

2513   I fear letting go of life

2514   and leaving the earth,

2515   I understand I will leave

2516   here one day with no

2517   intention to unwitness

2518   the torture that could not leave

2519   our home. I will forever engrain

2520   this experience into the most

2521   definitive end. Your love

2522   would heal that inability to

2523   continue and send me back

2524   again to save them.

2525   I wonder if I would

2526   feel with certainty the

2527   pain that they are

2528   forced to embody by then.

2529   I wonder if I feel it now

2530   despite being

2531   in a place of unawareness.

2532   I would not be confused

2533   if that were the case.

2534   I would not be

2535   longing for you

2536   as a way to collapse

2537   into that awareness

2538   with the enlightenment

2539   that you would give

2540   and the security of our

2541   oneness sustaining us.

2542   we should not take away pain

2543   even if that were our wish.

2544   I wonder what the world thinks

2545   love should do in an unconditional

2546   existence. I am at a crossroads

2547   now being confronted

2548   whether I am willing to die

2549   or commit to life. I will

2550   not know this will until

2551   I face death. I thought

2552   I was close enough through

2553   the state of health

2554 that weakens our emotional

2555 body through unrelentless

2556 masses of confusion without clarity.

2557 The thoughts I have I therefore cannot

2558 trust. The trust feels as if it is

2559 a necessity to not have when it would give

2560 the ultimate freedom that I do not crave.

2561 I wish to be bound by you

2562 even in uncertain times that blur

2563 my mind into a redundant

2564 state of comprehending nothing.

2565 I wonder if my mind

2566 numbs to show me

2567 what enlightenment will

2568 feel like in the future.

2569 I could be neglecting

2570 the pain of others by going

2571 back and forth in the

2572 pain of your absence.

2573 I may pretend that all

2574 beings are suffering in front of me

2575 and I must save them by wilful

2576 submission into a life without you.

2577   I cannot let you go.

2578   Letting go of you now would be

2579   choosing not to exceed

2580   the aching heart that is already

2581   at breaking point. I could break

2582   with you and then rise again

2583   once I disappear. I am

2584   meant to live a life

2585   of complete deprivation with

2586   the means to reach you but not be

2587   heard. I am only meant for this life

2588   and I am the sacrifice that you did not take.

2589   I am the result of all

2590   that may have gone wrong in your

2591   life with the belief that all

2592   which is wrong can be right

2593   though it will never feel right.

2594   My emotions invalidate me.

2595   They will send me into

2596   danger to find you

2597   or to comfort that then

2598   tells me that you are always here.

2599   I do not need to search.

₂₆₀₀ I need to belong.

₂₆₀₁ I need you to belong with me

₂₆₀₂ and I do not believe myself.

₂₆₀₃ I need to wake myself up from

₂₆₀₄ a dream that has not yet began.

₂₆₀₅ I need to live. I imagine you

₂₆₀₆ next to me now. I have you

₂₆₀₇ here. Here is where I desire to be.

₂₆₀₈ The pain of losing you is

₂₆₀₉ not what I desire. I must feel you

₂₆₁₀ here or feel you in the future.

₂₆₁₁ The question then is if I do

₂₆₁₂ not want pain then why do I

₂₆₁₃ immerse myself in it as if it is

₂₆₁₄ all that exists. I should look

₂₆₁₅ out into the future

₂₆₁₆ at the various actions that will

₂₆₁₇ lead me to you.

₂₆₁₈ The world is not denying me

₂₆₁₉ of this love. I have to understand

₂₆₂₀ that the world is part of me

₂₆₂₁ and not an outside force

₂₆₂₂ coming to take you away

2623   from me. You are here to protect

2624   the meticulous details of my love

2625   for you. I do not need to see

2626   you now. I rather need to see

2627   the means I have to reach you.

2628   The ways that we may

2629   unite are the tiny steps that will

2630   make our union happen.

2631   Our union will then be

2632   the beginning of another evolution.

2633   There are no ends here.

2634   There are patterns. I read books

2635   and I imagine you in the pages.

2636   I admire the idea of learning

2637   and growing our ambitions

2638   together. I feel we would

2639   inevitably think of ways

2640   to combine our thoughts

2641   and follow our passions

2642   together. You could take

2643   my lead and I would take yours.

2644   We would invent more outlets

2645   for our love. The mere invention

2646   would fulfil us. I do not need to be

2647   with you. I need to know

2648   with everything that exists in this universe

2649   and beyond that I always remain connected

2650   to you from the beginnings of existence

2651   until the ends of time stop moving

2652   and collapse into us both.

2653   I will keep existing.